T0197606

AuthorHouse™
1663 Liberty Drive
Bloomington, IN 47403
www.authorhouse.com
Phone: 833-262-8899

Because of the dynamic nature of the Internet, any web addresses or links contained in this book may have changed since publication and may no longer be valid. The views expressed in this work are solely those of the author and do not necessarily reflect the views of the publisher, and the publisher hereby disclaims any responsibility for them.

This book is printed on acid-free paper.

ISBN: 978-1-4490-2205-1 (sc)

Print information available on the last page.

Published by AuthorHouse 03/23/2022

authorHOUSE

This book is dedicated to my delightful granddaughter Samara and my adored sons Jeremiah and Zach, along with his wife krystal. I give special tribute to my five sisters Bertha, Helen, Lucille, Ruth, Alice, my three brothers Thomas, Isaiah, Roderick; I would also like to thank all of my nieces and my nephews. You have been my support system and the primary colors in my life.

The Author:

Lois Core Humphrey was born and raised in Birmingham, Alabama. She has spent many years writing for children's plays and puppet shows. The inspiration for this book came when her then 7 year old son asked some tough questions after a family friend passed away.

The Illustrator:

Tim Towns is a gifted artist who created the pictures that brought this story to life. His wife Debbie and daughter Jordan provided meaningful support for the project. Tim's intuitiveness contributed much to the warm Spirit of this book, and is greatly appreciated.

As Spirit awakened to the garden,

he glanced up, closed his eyes and allowed

the sun to bathe him with its warm rays.

"Thanks for shining on me," said Spirit.

"You're welcome", replied the sun. "I converted

some of that green stuff in your leaves to get

you going for the day".

"I can tell", said Spirit, "because everytime you convert

my chlorophyll, it's like giving me an energy pill".

"I just wish more creatures would get their energy

from me", added the sun.

"Well, I'm ready to start my day, and what a good

day it is", said Spirit, "just perfect for greeting

visitors and enjoying the garden".

"Hello Spirit," said the first visitor of the morning.

"Bumble Bee, what brings you here so early? asked Spirit.

Bee smiled, "Your delightful smell of course; it attracts me like a magnet. I can't wait to taste your sweet nectar!"

"Help yourself," said Spirit, as he allowed the bee to dance on his face. The visitor also pollinated the flower as he enjoyed his meal.

*S*pirit stretched his petals to the sky above, and extended his roots into the earth beneath.

"Settling in, are you?" asked the soil. "The leaves you shed last night enriched my health, for sure."

"Glad to do it," replied Spirit. "However, when I enrich you, weeds tend to grow as well. I don't want weeds in my garden."

"There will be a few weeds in every garden," declared the soil. "Don't let them grow too big or become too many, and you'll be fine - you will still bloom beautifully."

Suddenly, there was a brief rain that showered the garden.

"You really snuck up on me that time," said Spirit.

"Well, I do like to make unexpected visits," answered the rain.

"Indeed," said Spirit, "and even though I dread rainy days, I must thank you, because I always come through them stronger than before.
By the way, when you return home,
say hello to Cumulus Lou and Stratus Lee for me."

"Consider it done," replied his wet and wise friend.

As Spirit enjoyed his good life, a mild breeze flowed through it. "Hmm, that's nice," he said to the wind.

"Anytime," the wind replied. "Perhaps my breeze will help you spread your seeds around the garden. Creating new life is a gift, you know. It ensures that the garden will always be here."

"And what a lovely garden it is," declared Spirit. "I don't ever want to leave; I want to stay here forever."

"*N*othing here is forever,"
said the approaching butterfly.

"We all arrive in the garden, and experience it
in our own way. But, whether we have the misfortune
of leaving early in the morning, or blessed to leave
late at night… we all must leave. Just make sure
that your time in the garden fulfills a meaningful
purpose – for you and for the garden, before you leave."

"Leave? Not me," said Spirit.
"I'm going to stay here forever."

"Forever is a word," said the butterfly,
"a word that ignores Time…
and Time will not be ignored."

Spirit pondered these words, but had no reply.
The butterfly took a few minutes to rest on the flower,
then flew on her way.

*B*y the end of the season,

Spirit noticed that his stem drooped,

making him look as though his back was broken.

He was also alarmed that his petals had

turned brown, and they looked as though

they were crying.

The Wind and the Rain returned to comfort him.

"Listen Spirit," said the Rain, "to everything,

there is a season and a time to every purpose.

You have flourished during your season and,

in the time given, found and fulfilled your purpose.

Soon it will be time for you to leave the garden.

When you face Time - for the last time -

you can choose to rage against it like a storm,

or embrace it like a Spring shower."

"Either response is right," the Wind added,

"because the response you choose is a reflection of you."

"Although you will leave this beautiful place,

be glad that, because you received from it,

you will remember the garden.

And because you gave to it,

the garden will remember you."

*A*nd with that, the withering, yet strong, flower smiled at his life. He knew that he had received the ultimate gift. And like a child on Christmas Day, he had enjoyed it completely, despite knowing that it would end...
or perhaps because he knew it.

He also knew that even Time could not destroy such a wonderful *Spirit*. So, he allowed his eyes to close - and the garden to disappear.

*S*pirit slowly floated into a sea of peace, with clarity not known before. He had no sense of petals, nor stems or leaves, only the timeless energy of the oneness that was. Spirit surrendered himself to this moment of transition, and readied his eyes which remained closed.

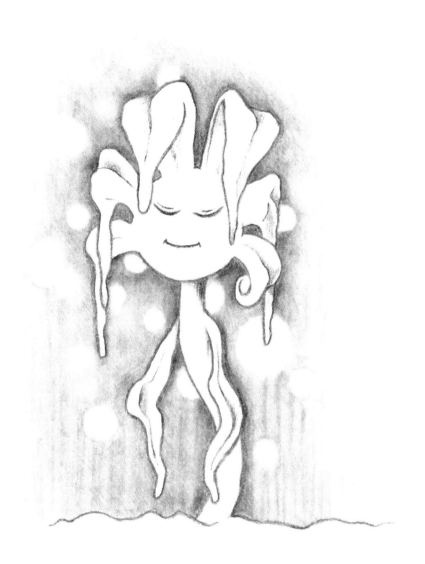

*T*hey opened again to endless fields of lavish blossoms like none he had ever seen. He heard enchanting music and giggling voices of praise. As Spirit surveyed the unspeakable beauty before him, he was amazed.

"Oh my," said Spirit,
"this is awesome, majestic beyond words...
and it **is** forever."

Printed in the United States
by Baker & Taylor Publisher Services